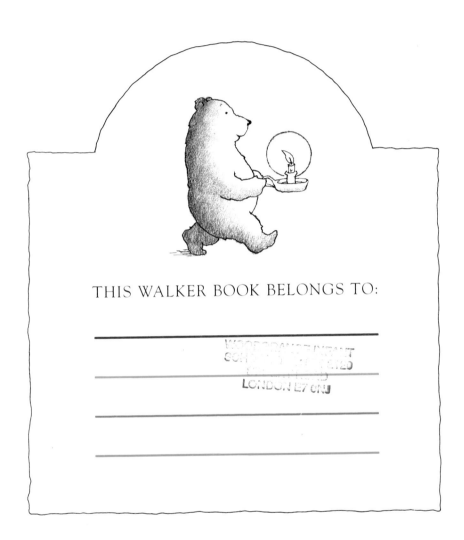

THIS WALKER BOOK BELONGS TO:

First published 1986 by Walker Books Ltd
87 Vauxhall Walk, London SE11 5HJ

This edition published 1998

Text © 1986 Allan Ahlberg
Illustrations © 1986 Colin McNaughton

This book has been typeset in New Baskerville Educational

Printed in Hong Kong

British Library Cataloguing in Publication Data
A catalogue record for this book is
available from the British Library.

ISBN 0-7445-6126-4 (hb)
ISBN 0-7445-6074-8 (pb)

BIG BAD PIG

Allan Ahlberg

Colin McNaughton

Big Bad Pig
Spotty Dog
In the Water

WALKER BOOKS

AND SUBSIDIARIES

LONDON • BOSTON • SYDNEY

Big Bad Pig

three little pigs

and a big bad wolf

three big pigs
and a big bad wolf

three little wolves

and a big bad pig

three little bad pigs

and a big wolf

three little pigs
and a big good wolf

Spotty Dog

fast
car

square
house

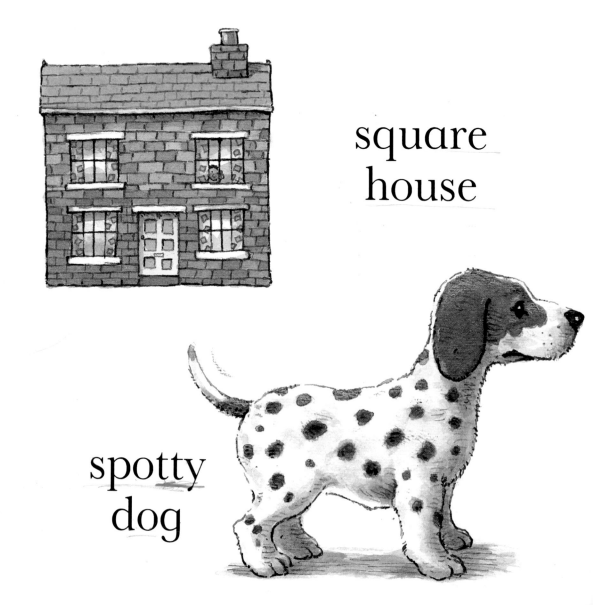

spotty
dog

square
car

spotty
house

fast
dog

fast house

In the Water

in the water

out of the water

in the jar

out of the jar

in the bucket

out of the bucket

in the bath

out of the bath

in the jar

out of the jar

in the water